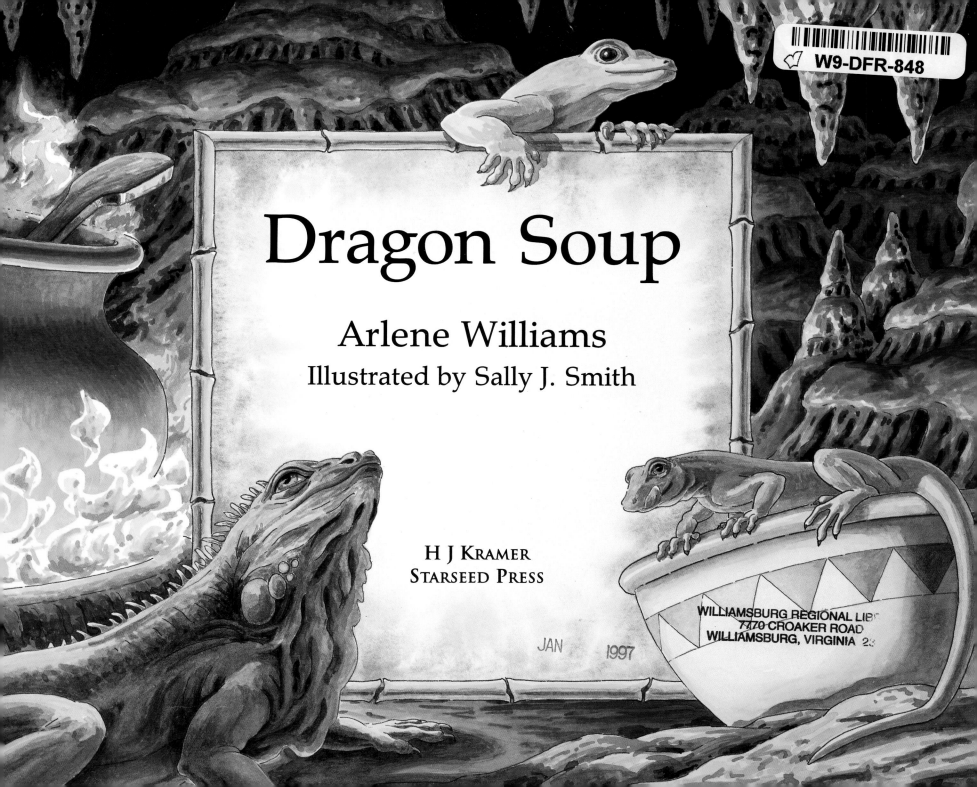

Dragon Soup

Arlene Williams
Illustrated by Sally J. Smith

H J Kramer
Starseed Press

Far away, in a land of jungles and mountains and mist, there once lived a beautiful girl named Tonlu. Every day, she worked in her father's fields of rice and beans, which were cut deeply into a steep mountainside like a set of giant steps. Tonlu's father called them dragon steps, for at the top of their mountain in a cave filled with splendid treasures lived the Cloud Dragons.

One evening, Tonlu and her brothers and sisters sat at the edge of a terrace, eating their supper and watching the people of the village far below move about like tiny ants.

"How I'd hate to live in the village," Tonlu said as she ate her soup.

"But there would be so much more to do in the village than here," argued Zan, her younger brother.

"Yes, but here you can look down the valley and over the low hills almost as far as the sea," Tonlu explained. "Down in the village, people see only the shadow of the mountains. I could never live there. I need to see far—very, very far."

Zan was about to argue back when he spotted a figure scurrying up the steep path toward their home. "It's the merchant," he said anxiously. "Why is *he* coming here?"

Tonlu stared at the tall, grim man. She answered slowly. "Father owes him money. That's why he has come."

The merchant was greeted solemnly by Tonlu's father, and the two men went inside the small house that was the family's home. On the terrace, the children waited, wondering what the visitor was saying to their father.

It wasn't long before the merchant left, and Tonlu's mother called the children in to sleep. Nothing was said about the merchant, but Tonlu could see the worry in her father's face, and when he kissed her good night, there were tears in his eyes.

Later that night, Zan shook Tonlu awake. "Come outside," he whispered as he pointed to the door.

Tonlu rose from her bed and followed Zan out to the edge of the terrace. "What's wrong?" she asked.

"I heard Mother and Father talking," Zan explained. "Father doesn't have the money to pay the merchant, and he has only two weeks to find enough. If he can't, he must give the farm to the merchant or . . . " Zan paused a moment, looking gravely at his sister. "Or he must let the merchant claim you for his bride."

"Oh, I couldn't marry *him!*" Tonlu cried out. "And I couldn't live down there in the village!"

"I know," Zan sighed. "But then we'll lose the farm."

"No, we won't," Tonlu said firmly. "I will pay the merchant."

Zan looked at her, bewildered. Then he realized his sister's plan, for she was staring through the darkness toward the top of the mountain. "No! It would be better to marry the merchant than to meet the Cloud Dragons."

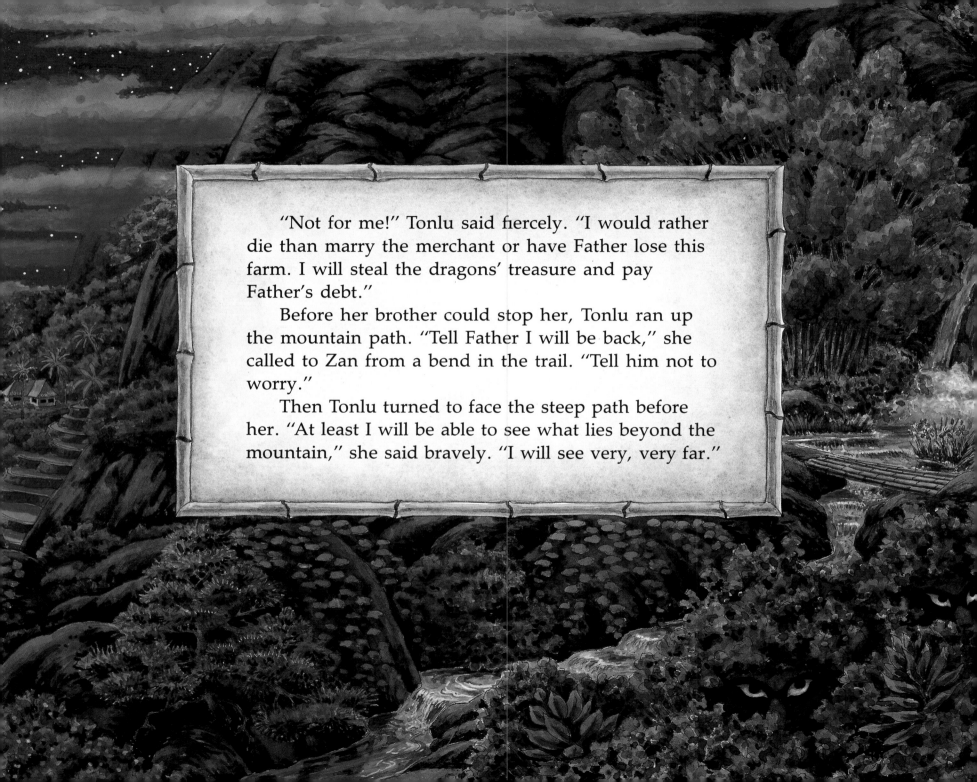

"Not for me!" Tonlu said fiercely. "I would rather die than marry the merchant or have Father lose this farm. I will steal the dragons' treasure and pay Father's debt."

Before her brother could stop her, Tonlu ran up the mountain path. "Tell Father I will be back," she called to Zan from a bend in the trail. "Tell him not to worry."

Then Tonlu turned to face the steep path before her. "At least I will be able to see what lies beyond the mountain," she said bravely. "I will see very, very far."

It was many hours later when Tonlu crept through the cold, dark mist of the mountain toward the mouth of a cave. Inside, she could see two huge dragons sitting before a crackling fire. One dragon was bright red with long, scaly wings. The other dragon had no wings but wore ropes of giant pearls around his blue-green neck.

Tonlu stared at the pearls. In the village, they would bring a fortune. "I only need one," she told herself. "Just one."

She curled up behind a boulder and waited.

At last the dragons fell asleep. Tonlu listened to their dreadful snores. Then she crept toward the blue-green dragon, stopping as he groaned and twitched in a fitful dream.

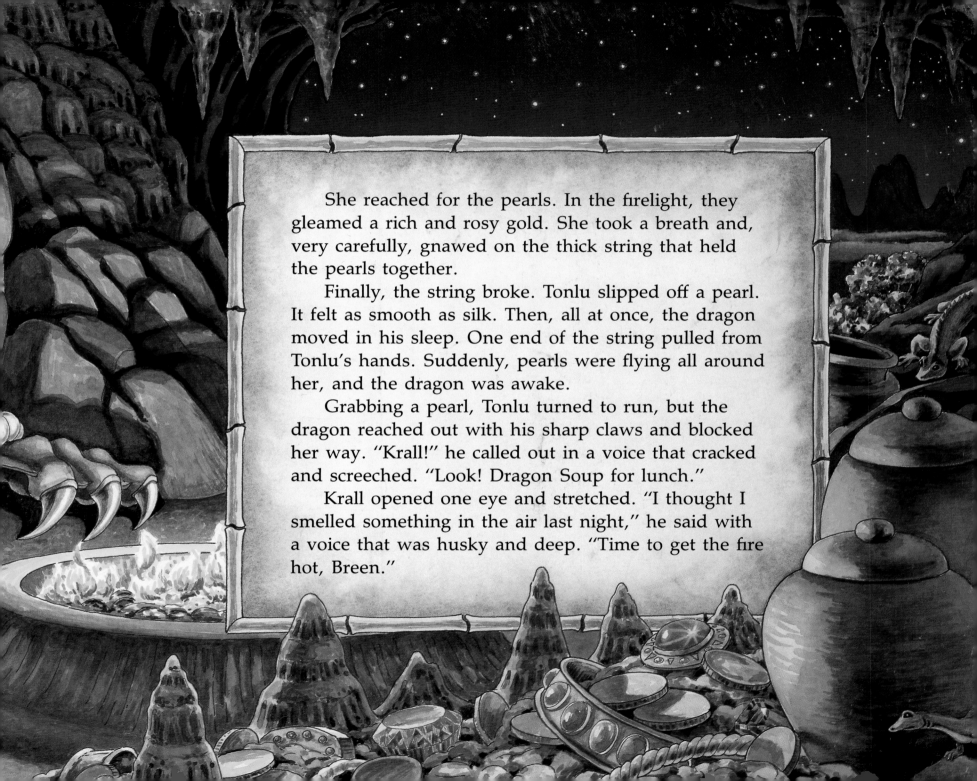

She reached for the pearls. In the firelight, they gleamed a rich and rosy gold. She took a breath and, very carefully, gnawed on the thick string that held the pearls together.

Finally, the string broke. Tonlu slipped off a pearl. It felt as smooth as silk. Then, all at once, the dragon moved in his sleep. One end of the string pulled from Tonlu's hands. Suddenly, pearls were flying all around her, and the dragon was awake.

Grabbing a pearl, Tonlu turned to run, but the dragon reached out with his sharp claws and blocked her way. "Krall!" he called out in a voice that cracked and screeched. "Look! Dragon Soup for lunch."

Krall opened one eye and stretched. "I thought I smelled something in the air last night," he said with a voice that was husky and deep. "Time to get the fire hot, Breen."

Breen took his captive and put her in a cage near the wall of the cave. "So you like stealing pearls?" he hissed.

Tonlu stared at the large iron pot Krall had placed over the fire. "I only wanted one," she whispered.

"Only one?" Breen cackled. "You thought I might not miss it?"

Then Breen placed a second pot of water over the fire. Soon the dragons were carefully adding herbs and spices from huge earthen jars to their own boiling brews.

Tonlu watched the dragons work with wide and fearful eyes. She wished she had never come to the dragons' cave.

Finally, Breen came toward her. Tonlu felt the heat of his fiery breath. "Soup's almost done. Are you ready to . . . choose?"

Tonlu stared at the dragon. "Choose? What do you mean?"

Breen snorted at the red dragon. "My brother and I can't agree on whose soup is better. His is much too spicy, but he complains mine is too sweet. So we've been waiting for a visitor to wander up the mountain and decide for us."

Krall rolled his fearsome eyes and commanded, "Choose which soup is better. Then we'll set you free."

"Free?" asked Tonlu. "And you won't put me in your soup?"

"Oh, heavens no!" shuddered Krall. "That would spoil it, I'm sure." Then he added with a gruesome wink, "Of course, if I lose, I might be tempted to try a new ingredient."

"That's not fair! You're cheating!" screamed Breen as he spat at Krall. Then the blue-green dragon leaned toward the cage. Tiny puffs of smoke swirled around Tonlu. "If you choose my soup, you can keep the pearl."

"No! Choose my soup, and I will fly you around the world on my back!" thundered the red dragon. "How would you like that?"

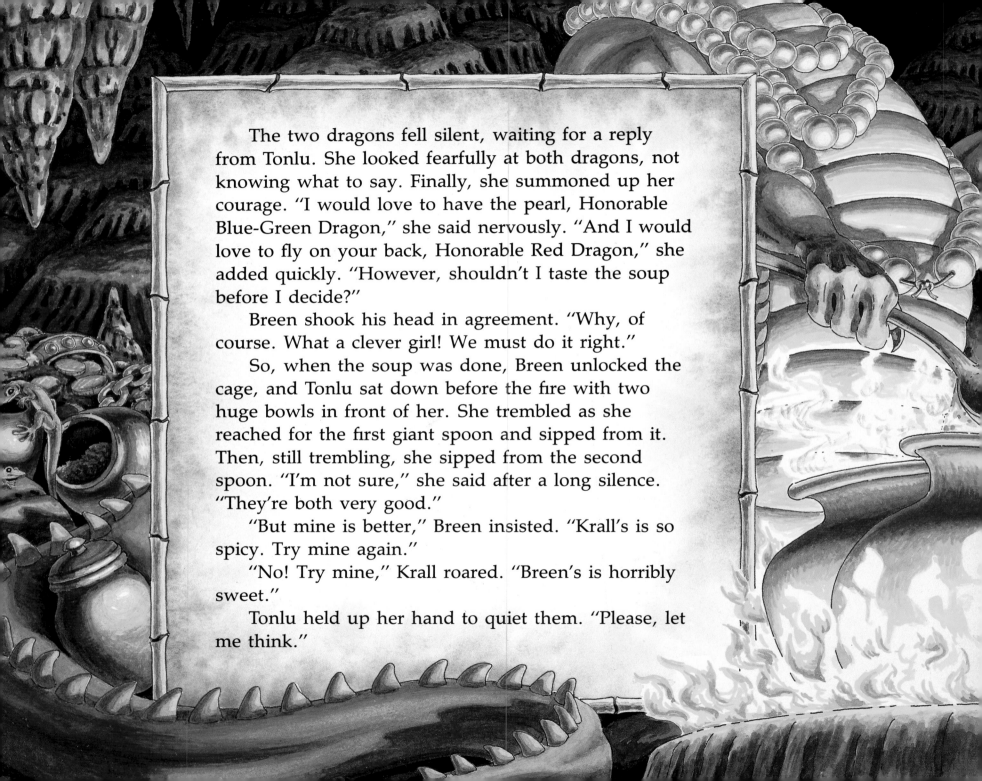

The two dragons fell silent, waiting for a reply from Tonlu. She looked fearfully at both dragons, not knowing what to say. Finally, she summoned up her courage. "I would love to have the pearl, Honorable Blue-Green Dragon," she said nervously. "And I would love to fly on your back, Honorable Red Dragon," she added quickly. "However, shouldn't I taste the soup before I decide?"

Breen shook his head in agreement. "Why, of course. What a clever girl! We must do it right."

So, when the soup was done, Breen unlocked the cage, and Tonlu sat down before the fire with two huge bowls in front of her. She trembled as she reached for the first giant spoon and sipped from it. Then, still trembling, she sipped from the second spoon. "I'm not sure," she said after a long silence. "They're both very good."

"But mine is better," Breen insisted. "Krall's is so spicy. Try mine again."

"No! Try mine," Krall roared. "Breen's is horribly sweet."

Tonlu held up her hand to quiet them. "Please, let me think."

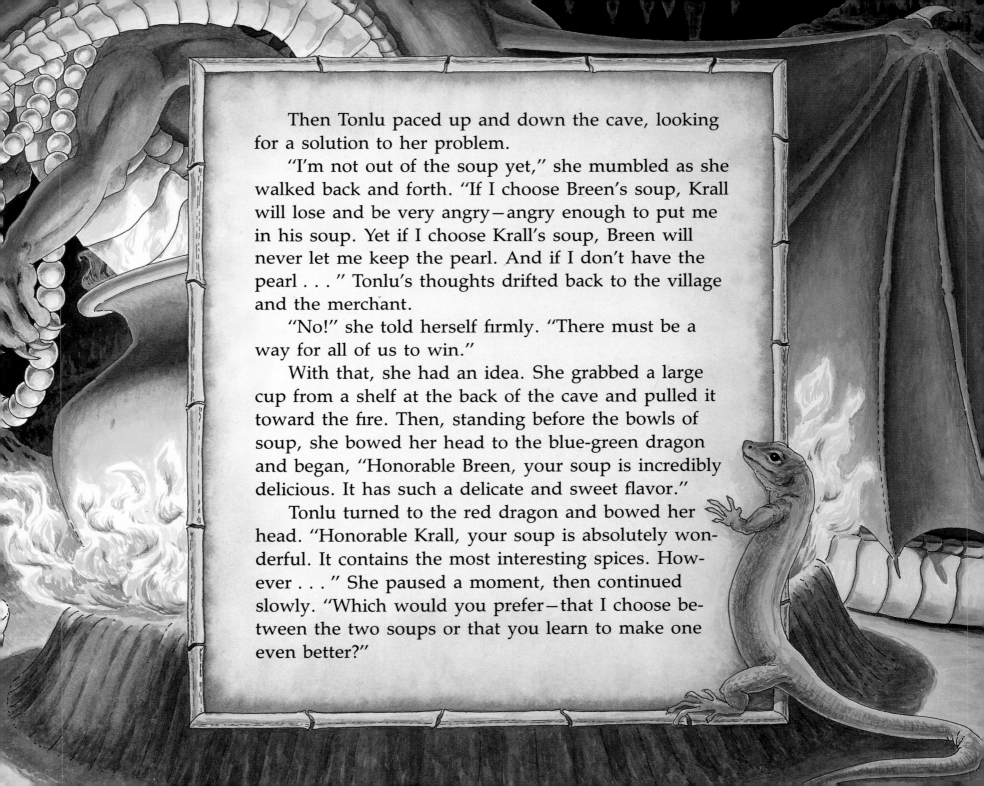

Then Tonlu paced up and down the cave, looking for a solution to her problem.

"I'm not out of the soup yet," she mumbled as she walked back and forth. "If I choose Breen's soup, Krall will lose and be very angry—angry enough to put me in his soup. Yet if I choose Krall's soup, Breen will never let me keep the pearl. And if I don't have the pearl . . ." Tonlu's thoughts drifted back to the village and the merchant.

"No!" she told herself firmly. "There must be a way for all of us to win."

With that, she had an idea. She grabbed a large cup from a shelf at the back of the cave and pulled it toward the fire. Then, standing before the bowls of soup, she bowed her head to the blue-green dragon and began, "Honorable Breen, your soup is incredibly delicious. It has such a delicate and sweet flavor."

Tonlu turned to the red dragon and bowed her head. "Honorable Krall, your soup is absolutely wonderful. It contains the most interesting spices. However . . . " She paused a moment, then continued slowly. "Which would you prefer—that I choose between the two soups or that you learn to make one even better?"

Breen shook his head. "There couldn't be a soup sweeter than mine."

Krall flapped his wings. "Nor spicier than mine."

"Perhaps not," said Tonlu carefully. "But I can tell you a way to make the best soup in the Kingdom of the Cloud Dragons. Do you want to know how?"

Both dragons nodded their heads eagerly.

Tonlu smiled. All at once, she dipped a spoon into Krall's bowl of soup and poured it into the cup. Then she added a spoonful of Breen's soup and stirred the two together. She took a sip and announced triumphantly, "Mixed together, they make the most delightful soup I have ever tasted."

Both dragons stared at her, not knowing what to say. Finally, Breen cleared his throat. "But nobody won," he grumbled.

Tonlu smiled her most radiant smile. "On the contrary, both of you won. Now you have a soup you can enjoy together."

"Together?" roared Krall.

"Taste it yourself," Tonlu said as she pointed to the cup.

Breen took a sip. "Why, yes. I like it," he declared. "It's sweet and spicy at the same time." Then he frowned and added quickly, "But not too spicy."

Krall took a sip. He winked at Breen. "And it's not too sweet," he rumbled. Then he took Breen's pot of soup, mixed it with his own, and poured himself a huge bowl.

"How can we ever thank you?" Breen said gratefully as he watched his brother gulp down the soup.

"Set me free," replied Tonlu. "And let me keep your pearl."

"Certainly." The dragon bowed. "Is that all?"

Tonlu turned to Krall. "I have always wanted to see far beyond the mountain. Perhaps you would still be willing to give me a ride on your back?"

"Clever girl!" the dragon thundered as he licked his spoon happily. "I would be honored."

Without a moment's hesitation, Tonlu gathered up her pearl and climbed on the red dragon's back. They took off into the sky, rising above the mist that clung to the mountaintop.

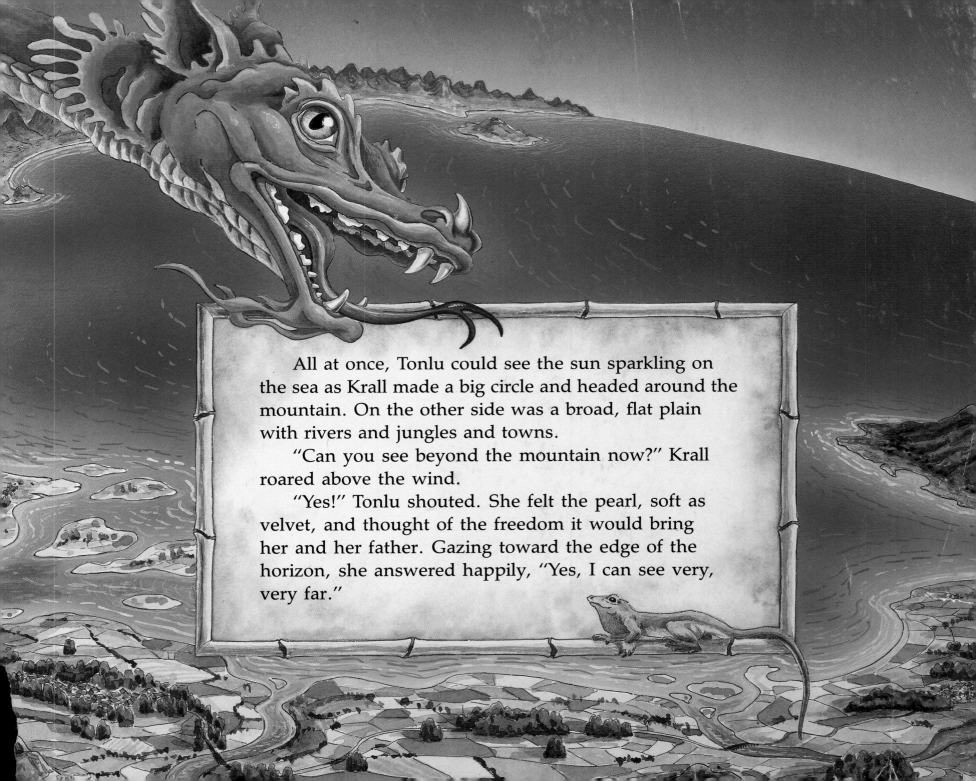

All at once, Tonlu could see the sun sparkling on the sea as Krall made a big circle and headed around the mountain. On the other side was a broad, flat plain with rivers and jungles and towns.

"Can you see beyond the mountain now?" Krall roared above the wind.

"Yes!" Tonlu shouted. She felt the pearl, soft as velvet, and thought of the freedom it would bring her and her father. Gazing toward the edge of the horizon, she answered happily, "Yes, I can see very, very far."

Text copyright © 1996 by Arlene Williams.
Illustrations copyright © 1996 by Sally J. Smith.

H J Kramer Inc
P.O. Box 1082
Tiburon, CA 94920

Library of Congress Cataloging-in-Publication Data

Williams, Arlene.
  Dragon soup / Arlene Williams : illustrated by Sally J. Smith.
    p. cm.
  Summary: When Tonlu tries to steal a pearl from the Cloud Dragons' treasure in order to help her father pay his debts, she finds herself resolving a dispute about soup recipes.
  ISBN 0–915811–63–4 : $15.95
  [1. Dragons—Fiction. 2. Soups—Fiction. 3. Cooperativeness—Fiction.] I. Smith, Sally J., 1954–   ill. II. Title.
PZ7.W655856Dr 1995
[Fic]—dc20   94–23216
                                                                    CIP
                                                                    AC

Editor: Nancy Grimley Carleton
Art Directors: Linda Kramer and Dick Schuettge
Book Production: Schuettge and Carleton
Composition: Classic Typography
Printed in Singapore
10 9 8 7 6 5 4 3 2 1